# Not a Chance

## Robert Gott

/

sundance

A Haights Cross Communications Company

 a black dog book

Published by Sundance Publishing
P.O. Box 1326, 234 Taylor Street, Littleton, MA 01460
800-343-8204

Copyright © text Black Dog Productions

First published 1999 as Phenomena by
Horwitz Martin
A Division of Horwitz Publications Pty Ltd
55 Chandos St., St. Leonards NSW 2065 Australia

Exclusive United States Distribution: Sundance Publishing

ISBN 0-7608-8039-5

# Contents

4

# Author's Note

I've met a few people in my life who seem to be followed around by bad luck. Something goes wrong for them almost every day. A friend of mine bought a new car and crashed it on the way home from the dealer. Then, driving it home from the repair shop, a car ran into the back of it. Driving it home after getting it repaired a second time, he had a flat tire. We all began to think that the car was cursed. I refused to drive anywhere with him.

It wasn't just his car that was cursed. He's had four cats in the past five years. Two of them were hit by cars, and the other two died of some strange disease.

I thought it would be fun to write about someone whose whole life is a series of mishaps but who remains positive and cheerful through it all. Roscoe wins in the end, and I suppose that's the point, isn't it? If you hang in there, things will turn out for the best.

*Robert Gott has never been particularly lucky. But he has always been interested in people who experience extraordinary luck.*

# Chapter 1

# What's in a Name?

_Fact_: The most common surname in both Great Britain and the United States is Smith. In Great Britain, Jones is next. In the United States, Johnson is next.

ROSCOE BOULDER. That's my name. Roscoe. Boulder. I hate it. I hate Roscoe, and I hate Boulder, and I really hate the two of them together. I don't have a middle name, which is just as well, because I'd probably hate that, too. I suppose I should be used to it by now. My dad's always telling me that I should be proud of it.

"You are the 15th Roscoe Boulder," he says, "and I am the 14th. Many fine men have owned that name before you."

Don't get me wrong. I like my dad. We get along really well. Usually. It's just that I get sick of hearing about our glorious family, especially since I can't see

what's so glorious about it. All of my ancestors look like losers to me.

"No, Roscoe," my dad would say. "They struggled against the odds, but remember the family motto, 'Get up and try again.' They did get up and try again, and they were great men."

"And they were married to great women," added my mother.

Yeah, well, let me tell you about one of these great men, and you can make up your own mind. I heard this story from my mother. She was trying to explain the Boulder jinx to me.

She doesn't believe in the jinx. My dad sort of doesn't, but I've heard him say that if something is going to go wrong, you don't have to look far to find a Roscoe Boulder. It's certainly true that Dad is accident-prone. He knows all of the people who work in the emergency room at the hospital by

*jinx: Bad luck.*

their first names. In fact, he knows them so well that he even gets Christmas cards from them.

M om was trying to reassure me one day that the whole thing about a jinx was nonsense. She said she could tell me a story to prove it. I felt there was something I needed to know before she got started, so I interrupted her. "Have you had the same number of accidents as Dad?"

"No one has had as many accidents as your father," she said. Then she realized that she'd said the wrong thing. "What I mean is that your father is just a bit vague, and he hits his head sometimes, or falls into holes. It's one of the things I love about him."

"He broke his arm sharpening a pencil," I said.

"Yes, well, that could happen to anybody, given the right set of circumstances."

"What were the circumstances?"

Mom paused and then admitted, "Well, actually he was just sharpening a pencil. Oh dear, I'm not doing a very good job of reassuring you about the jinx, am I? I'm really trying not to frighten you."

It hadn't occurred to me, until the word "frighten" was used, that there was anything about my family

that could frighten me. Now, I wasn't so sure.

Mom must have noticed a look of panic on my face—she's very observant. She started to tell me a story about how silly it was to believe in something as dumb as a jinx.

"In about 1780," she said, "there was quite a famous Roscoe Boulder. He was a sailor and an explorer—a traveler really. He loved the sea and went to many strange places—strange for those days, that is. He kept a journal in which he wrote over and over again that he believed in the Boulder jinx. He thought it was just a matter of time before it affected him badly.

"His father—who fainted and fell into a bowl of soup and drowned—had drummed into him that all of the Roscoe Boulders were jinxed. Nothing dramatic happened to this Roscoe Boulder, the traveler, but he still believed in the jinx. It was this belief that destroyed him.

"On one voyage, he took along his young wife and their baby, a boy named Roscoe. They were very happy together. The Boulders always marry successfully. They marry strong women who don't mind the sight of blood. However, a few weeks after

they set sail, a terrible calm
settled over the ocean. The ship
didn't move for days. There
was not a breath of wind, and
the people on board thought
that they might go mad with
the heat. After a week, the
drinking water supply began to
run low.

"Roscoe got it into his head
that the ship was in trouble
because he was on board. He
thought that he had somehow
made the wind die. He thought
that if he left, everything would
be all right again. He loved
his wife and baby. In fact, he
loved them so much that he couldn't stand the
thought of them suffering the terrible thirst that
would soon overtake them.

"Late one night, he crept up on deck, lowered a
dinghy, and rowed away toward the horizon. No one
ever saw him again. The next day, the wind rose and
blew the ship to safety. Coincidence? Of course. If
he'd waited, the wind would have arrived. So what
do you think?"

"He sounds like a total loser," I replied.

Mom knitted her brows when I said that.

"No, Roscoe. He was a brave man who made a great sacrifice. The only problem was, his reasons for doing it were all wrong."

Maybe I was missing something. But it seemed to me that here was a guy who left his wife and baby to fend for themselves because of a stupid superstition.

"Like I said, Mom, he sounds like a loser."

She gave in. "Yes, well, maybe that's what you become if you believe in something as silly as a jinx. I'm glad we had this little chat, Roscoe, but it's time for me to help your father change his bandage."

I't's funny how some things creep up on you. Until the word "jinx" was mentioned, it never occurred to me to think of myself as being under an ancient curse. I didn't believe in it at all, but something started to nag at me. Every time I fell over—and I fall over a lot—I started to say, "There's that jinx again." I was being funny. I know it's not hilarious or anything, but I thought at the time that it was funny.

Before long though, I felt myself accepting the possibility that there might be something to the jinx. I knew, even as I was thinking this, that it was

ridiculous. But I just couldn't help myself. One thing was certain, I was going to stay very close to shore. If the Roscoe Boulders of this world are prone to rowing off beyond the horizon, you won't catch me in a boat.

The more I thought about the superstition, the more interested I became in my family's history. I wanted to know about the other Roscoes lurking in the family tree.

But the family stuff had to be put on hold for a while. My most pressing concern now was the swim meet. I love swimming, and I was certain to win the 100-meters freestyle. No one was as fast as I was.

There was another concern, though—a girl named Claire Moore. I'd been in the same class as Claire for a couple of years, but I'd never really paid much attention to her. In fact, until recently, I'd never even looked at her too closely. She was just another girl. So I really never paid her much attention.

I'm not sure how it happened. But one day I was aware that she had brilliant blue eyes and dark, curly hair. It was long, and she used to gather it in both hands, push it behind her ears, and flick it. She did this a lot. My friends thought that she was a snob. This was because whenever she turned those

> **prone**: Likely to act in a certain way.

brilliant blue eyes in our direction, she seemed to be looking down her nose at us. She had a way of making us feel like insects. She would flick her hair as if to dismiss us. Then she'd stick her chin in the air and glide off with her friends.

D on't panic. This isn't going to turn into a soppy love story. I didn't even like her, honestly I didn't, but I found out one day that she actually liked me. I knew this because in class she slipped me a note saying that her friends thought that I was okay. I don't know much about girls. But I know that if the friends think you're okay it really means that the girl thinks you're okay. One other thing that I knew about girls was that they didn't like being teased.

On the day of the swim meet, I had butterflies in my stomach. I knew that there was no way that I could be beaten. But in the back of my mind I had a lurking worry about the jinx. What if it kicked in today? I wished that I'd never heard about it.

Before the race, Claire came up to me to wish me good luck. I was embarrassed because my friends were watching.

"Can I look after your watch?" she asked.

"Sure," I said, without thinking. Then I began to

worry that she might think that this meant we were
going steady or engaged or something.

On the starting blocks, I was focused and cool. I
watched the water in front of me, imagining the point
of entry and waiting for the sound of the pistol. My
only competition was a kid named Barney. He was
tall, but he never trained. The others were all slow. I
was the only one who took swimming seriously.

At the sound of the pistol, I launched myself into
the pool. It was a beautiful dive. It felt perfect, as if
there had been hardly any splash. I moved through
the water like an object with a razor-sharp edge.
When I touched the wall and raised my head, I knew
that I had won by a big margin. I let out a whoop of
triumph. I was excited. So much for the jinx. I can
only explain what I did next as being the result of a
mixture of high excitement and relief.

I'm normally quite shy. But I leaped out of that pool
and ran past the spectators, waving my arms and doing
a sort of victory dance. At first, I couldn't understand
why they were laughing so loudly. My dance wasn't
that funny. Then I looked down and realized that I'd
lost my bathing suit during the swim. I can't begin to
describe to you what it feels like to be stark naked in
front of the entire school.

"I'll never live it down," I said to my parents that evening.

"Of course you will," said Dad. "You have to turn this to your advantage. No one can do that better than a Boulder. It's in the blood."

"The first Olympics were run in the nude," said my mother helpfully.

I forgot to mention that Claire Moore gave my watch back to me at the end of the day. She didn't say anything. But the look on her face told me that if she ever thought we were engaged, it was now definitely off. Oddly, I was a little disappointed.

# Chapter 2
# Stressed Out

IMAGINE IF IT had been you running around in front of everyone with nothing on. How would you like to face your class the next day? If I'd had my way, I would have changed schools. Or maybe even moved to another city, or even another country. Dad said that this was a very Roscoe Boulder situation and that I had to run right at it rather than away from it. That was easy for him to say.

"It's like falling off a horse, son. You have to get right back on or you'll lose your nerve."

I couldn't see what horseback riding had to do with my situation.

I'd like to think that walking into that classroom was courageous. It wasn't though. You see, I had no choice. I had meant to get there early so that I would be the first to arrive. That way, people would enter in dribs and drabs, and I could deal with their ridicule one-on-one.

Dad drove me to school, and he ran into the back of someone's car at the lights. That held us up, and I was late. When I arrived, the whole class was already in their seats. So I walked in to a chorus of wolf-whistles and snickers. Our teacher hadn't arrived yet, so they had a field day. I wanted the earth to swallow me.

Then something surprising happened. John Watson, the biggest troublemaker and the coolest kid in the class, said, "That was wicked, Roscoe. You should have seen the look on Mrs. Jackson's face. Some stunt."

I was so busy being embarrassed that it took me a moment to understand what he was saying. Then it dawned on me. Watto thought that I'd lost my bathing suit on purpose, as a joke. Before I had a chance to agree, Mr. Harrold arrived and everyone shut up. Halfway through the class, Roger Tumblo leaned forward and whispered, "Hey, that was really cool."

The most amazing thing about this whole episode was that Dad had been right. Things are never as bad as you think they're going to be. All of my friends thought that what had happened was hilarious. I actually went up in their estimation.

By the end of that first day, I felt like I had become

a legend. I had told the story over and over. Each time my role in it became more dramatic. I made up stuff about wearing a bathing suit one size too big so it would come off easily. I made it sound like a very well-planned operation.

For weeks afterward, when something funny happened at school, people would say, "Yeah, it was funny, but not nearly as funny as what Roscoe did." It was like I had out-dared them all.

I couldn't help myself. I had always been fairly quiet. I wasn't a dweeb, but I wasn't a rebel either. Now everyone thought that I was unpredictable, maybe even a little dangerous. Everyone, that is, except Claire.

"You're soooo childish. Such a stupid boy," she said as she passed me in the hallway. She said "boy" as if it were the dirtiest word in the language. One of her friends added, "Claire hates you."

Claire could have told me that herself. She was right there. That's not how girls operate, though. The look on Claire's face certainly indicated that she was in complete agreement with her friend. I just couldn't figure out what she was so mad about.

See, I told you this wasn't going to be a love story. Claire would call it more of a hate story. Every day after that, she snubbed me or made some comment. Once, I caught her and her friends giggling over a piece of paper.

I was obviously meant to catch them because when they got up and moved away, they left the paper behind. I looked at it, just like I was supposed to, and there was a drawing of me on it. I'm not going to tell you what the drawing was, but it was nasty. It wasn't well drawn, either. It didn't look anything like me. I only knew it was me because . . . no, never mind.

Anyway, she became a real pain. She hassled me and made my life miserable. All of my friends said that I should just ignore her, that she was just a stuck-up girl. But she had a way of annoying me that I didn't know how to deal with. I especially didn't like it when she said things out loud about me in public. I decided to get some advice.

I didn't want to just come right out and tell my parents that I was being stressed out by a girl. I mean, how lame. I especially didn't want to say it

was Claire Moore. My parents were friendly with her parents. They saw each other quite often. I thought I'd approach the subject in a roundabout manner.

"How did you and Dad meet?" I asked Mom.

"I fell in love with your father the first time I met him, Roscoe. I ran over him in my car. Well, I knocked him down at an intersection. Nothing serious. He got up and smiled at me. He said that it was quite all right, that there was no harm done, that it was entirely his fault. When he walked away, I noticed that his pants were torn at the knee. I fell in love with an accident victim, and I've never regretted it."

Having heard this story, I had no idea how to introduce my little problem. I was depending on Mom saying something like, "Why do you ask?" Then I could say that there was this girl who was behaving oddly. And I was just wondering if she really meant it when she said that she hated me.

Mom got this faraway look in her eye, as if she was remembering the day she ran over my father. So I left her to her memories and found Dad.

Dad was working out in the shed, which was always risky. Mom used to say that when Dad went out to the shed, she never knew what time dinner would be. Sometimes he would end up getting stitches in the emergency room at the hospital. Once, he dropped a big lump of wood on his foot, and he was in a cast for three weeks.

When I interrupted him, he was reading a manual on how to work the new lathe he had bought. He thought he was something of a wood carver. He wasn't bad, I suppose. But how many pieces of wood in the shape of an apple does one family need?

Dad's shed wasn't just a little box at the back of the yard. It had two rooms. One was the workroom, and the other was a spare room with a bed and fridge in it. There was a bit of junk in this room, but people would stay in it when the house was crowded.

This happened around Christmas time when Mom's three sisters and their husbands and their kids came to stay. All of my cousins are younger than I am, except for Paul, who is exactly the same age. We were born in different cities but on the same day and practically at the same time. How weird is that? But there's no room for his story here. Maybe one day he'll get around to writing it down.

I came right out and told Dad that I was being hassled by a girl. I didn't want him going off into

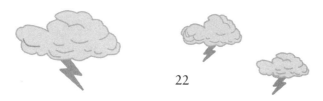

some dream world like Mom. He nodded his head sympathetically and said that in his opinion she had a crush on me.

"She's got a funny way of showing it," I said.

"If your name wasn't Roscoe Boulder, I'd agree with you. But this whole affair has to be looked at in that light."

This Roscoe Boulder business was really annoying.

"Dad," I said impatiently, "what's the deal with this Roscoe Boulder stuff?"

"It's not stuff, Roscoe." He looked concerned. "It's how it is, that's all. Let me show you something."

He went into the next room and brought back a large, leather-bound photo album.

"It's time you had a look at this," he said.

He blew dust from the cover and opened it. Inside were pages and pages of photographs of families and individuals. The pictures on the first pages were sepia. Then they became black and white, then washed-out color, and finally bright, recent color. As Dad turned the pages, he pointed out the various Roscoe Boulders.

There was my great-great-great-grandfather,

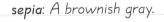
*sepia*: A brownish gray.

photographed in 1890. He was wearing an eye patch. On other pages, there were Roscoe Boulders with their arms in slings. Roscoe Boulders on crutches. And one Roscoe Boulder bandaged from head to foot.

"I'll tell you about him when you get a little older," Dad said.

"This looks like a photographic history of injury management practices," I said.

"That's the point, Roscoe. No one knows why it is, but the Roscoe Boulders of this world seem to be accident-prone. If you're a Roscoe Boulder, you have to learn to live with the fact that things will never turn out exactly as you expect. You don't need to worry about this, Roscoe, just be aware of it. Always remember, it's not what happens to you, it's how you deal with it that counts. Boulders always believe that things will work out for the best, even though history may be against us."

I think Dad thought that he had explained things so clearly that my question about Claire Moore had been answered. He closed the album and said that he hoped that our discussion had sorted out my problem. It hadn't. Although I admit that when I went back into the house, I did feel as though

something had been worked out.

I can't explain it, but looking through that album had made me stop worrying about the horrible words Claire Moore had said to me. Was there something to this Roscoe Boulder stuff after all? I didn't have much time to ponder. I heard Dad yell, "Ouch!" Then I saw him hurry into the bathroom to put a bandage on the thumb he had struck with a hammer. At least dinner was served at the usual time that night.

# Chapter 3

# The Boulders in History

> _Fact_: The oldest known books are actually clay blocks. The Babylonians scratched information about business dealings into clay.

I MUST HAVE shown more interest in Dad's photo album than I realized. When I went to bed that night, there was an enormous book on the end of my bed with a note attached.

"Roscoe," the note read, "this is the most precious object I own. It is _The Chronicle of the Roscoe Boulders,_ and it covers all of their lives from the first to the most recent—that's you. Your story isn't here yet because it is the responsibility of each Roscoe to write his story down when he is ready to do so. My story isn't here yet either. I have started it, but until it's finished, I won't add it.

"This book has been all around the world and has been kept and protected for more than 400 years by

the Boulders. With each generation it grows bigger. One day, this book will be yours. Preserving it is a big responsibility. Some of the pages are fragile. Whenever a history is added, the book must be rebound. The cover is not original. We don't know what happened to the first cover. This cover was designed by Roscoe Boulder in 1824. I hope that reading these stories will help you realize your position in our great tradition. Dad."

It was a beautiful book. It was the thickest and heaviest book I had ever seen. It looked like one of those magician's books you see in the movies or in cartoons. Only it didn't contain spells. I carried it to my desk and opened the cover. On the first page, in beautiful lettering, were the words "Being the glorious history of Roscoe Boulder and all those who come after."

The first pages weren't made of paper. They were made of a kind of skin called vellum, and I couldn't read the writing on them. It was in English, but all of the letters ran together and the handwriting was impossible to decipher. There

> **decipher**: Make out the meaning of.

were lots of pages like this, and some of them had little paintings on them. One was of a man falling from a horse, so I figured this was a picture of an ancestor.

It wasn't until about halfway through the book that I was able to read the words. I noticed a page that had obviously been scribbled quickly. It was dated June 25, 1876. To my astonishment, it had been written at the Battle of Little Bighorn.

*If Lieutenant-Colonel Custer will listen to my advice, we will attack the Sioux now while the element of surprise is with us. Our scouts have just returned from the Little Bighorn River. They report that the Sioux have gathered there and that their numbers are not great. Custer is uncertain. He has instructions to meet General Terry at the junction of the Bighorn and Little Bighorn rivers. But if we do this, we will miss our chance for glory. Imagine if this regiment, my regiment, of our brave Seventh United States Cavalry, were to subdue the Sioux and the Cheyenne. I think he will listen, because I think he is a vain man who will not turn his back on fame.*

*I can't believe it! Custer agreed with me that an attack would succeed. I now know that these are the last words I will ever write. We are surrounded and outnumbered. We have made a terrible mistake and we . . .*

The manuscript broke off here, but there was a note printed in a neat hand on the bottom. It read, *Delivered to me, Mrs. Roscoe Boulder, by Lieutenant George Linden, who found it among the belongings of my late, lamented husband, Roscoe*

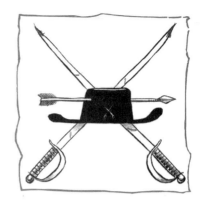

*Boulder. May our son one day know what a brave and decent man his father was.*

I was fascinated by this story. A Roscoe Boulder at the Battle of Little Bighorn! How incredible and how typical that he should give such bad advice.

I went to sleep that night with images of Little Bighorn swirling around in my head. Was there a picture of this Roscoe in the album? No. The first of those pictures was from about 1890. There was probably one of his son or grandson. Suddenly my whole attitude about my name had changed. I wanted to know more. I'm not sure that I was proud of my ancestors, but I was certainly interested to learn about them.

The incident at the swim meet began to fade as the weeks went by. My sudden rush of popularity had leveled off, and I settled back into my usual friendships. Claire Moore still snubbed me, but I didn't care. At least, I tried to give the impression that I didn't care. I suppose I must have cared because some weird force made me keep trying to impress her. I always ended up being embarrassed, but I didn't seem to learn. The worst, the very worst, attempt happened on a school field trip.

# Chapter 4
# Up to My Neck in It

*Fact*: Throughout the world, in any one year, 70 million sharks are killed by humans, while only 10 humans are killed by sharks.

I WAS LOOKING forward to this field trip. We were going to walk a long way into a fairly rugged wilderness area near the coast and then set up our two-person tents. This sounded exciting, but there was a catch. We didn't get to choose the person we shared the tent with.

Our school had this bizarre policy of making us share a tent with a person outside of our group of friends. This was supposed to bring the class closer together. All of our names were put into a hat. So who we ended up with became a lucky draw. Of course, the girls and boys had separate hats. Anyway, that's how I ended up with Peter Spike.

Believe me, sharing a tent with Peter Spike doesn't

do anything for class morale. Well, that's not true. The fact that I ended up sharing with him did wonders for everyone else's morale.

I decided to make the most of it. To the best of my knowledge he didn't smell or anything. It was just that he was stupid and nasty.

"Hey, Boulder," he said, "you better not snore or I'll thump you."

The walk into our campsite was long. After a while, the pack and the tent (I ended up carrying the tent) began to feel as heavy as lead. Everyone else seemed to be coping okay, so I didn't dare complain. I was sure the girls' packs must have been lighter. (They weren't. I checked later when no one was looking.)

We had been dropped off at a parking lot by the bus and were due back there in three days. I suppose the walk was only about four hours, but it felt like a

death march. Peter Spike was useless. He refused to help put up the tent. He knew I wouldn't argue. I wasn't scared of him. I just couldn't be bothered arguing. Besides, Spike could barely tie his shoelaces, let alone wrestle with a tent.

The campsite was great. It was in a clearing among low-growing scrub. There were a few tall trees. But we were so close to the ocean that scrub was mainly what grew here. We could hear the ocean beyond the dunes. We could smell it, too. The air was sharp with the tang of salt. We were told that we were not allowed to begin exploring until the camp had been set up properly. A latrine had to be dug and fires prepared. All tents had to be pitched and the gear stowed correctly. We were given one hour to set up.

At the sound of the whistle, the class came together to listen to the two gym teachers give instructions. Mr. Smith and Ms. Baker were young, but they both had bad tempers. So most of the kids tried not to cross them. Mr. Harrold, our teacher, had come along, too. I'd never seen him without a tie, so it was weird to see him in shorts and a tee shirt. It was even weirder to see him

> latrine: A toilet.

in a bathing suit. I wished I hadn't.

Mr. Smith explained that swimming was forbidden unless either he or Ms. Baker was watching. There was a beach beyond the dunes and there was an undertow. I saw several kids raise their eyes at each other as if to say, "Yeah, right."

"Don't raise your eyes like that, Jeremy," said Mr. Smith. "I don't really care whether you drown or not. But your parents might be upset and they might sue me. I don't want to end up in court because you've done something stupid. Understand?"

"Yes, sir," he said reluctantly, all the while mentally choosing among a number of stupid options.

As it turned out, the person who won the prize for

doing the stupidest thing that day was me. I was standing in the shallows with a whole lot of people. We were getting our ankles used to the chill of the water before plunging in.

Claire was there with her friends. She pushed her hair back behind her ears and looked at

me nastily. "Nice tan," she said.

I didn't have a tan, but I wasn't the only one. Most of the kids were untanned.

"Tanned skin is dead skin," I said.

"That's odd. You don't have a tan, but you do have dead skin."

I blushed. Of course it wasn't true, but recently Claire had found ways of getting to me. Once, I would have just ignored her, but now I dreaded her insults. Worse, I actually wanted her to like me. To cover my embarrassment, I said to my friends, "If you dig a hole in the sand, I'll let you bury me up to my neck."

Why would anybody say this? When I think about it now, the only explanation I can come up with is that I must have thought that Claire would be impressed. Why would a girl be impressed with a boy just because he jumps into a hole and invites someone else to bury him? Boys have no idea.

Maybe the very first person ever to bungee jump was my great-grandfather. It's the sort of thing

**bungee:** *The elastic cord used in bungee jumping.*

a Boulder might do to impress someone. There must have been a girl nearby. Imagine it . . .

Person with Great-Grandfather Boulder: "All right. I'm going to tie this long piece of elastic around your ankles, and then you're going to jump off this bridge. Okay?"

Great-Grandfather Boulder: "Are you sure this is safe?"

Person: "I don't know. We'll find out. Ready?"

Great-Grandfather Boulder: "AAAAAHHHhhhhhhhh . . ."

My friends couldn't wait to dig the hole. I've never seen them work so fast. They dug it where the sand was moist but away from the water. I hopped in, like an idiot, and they dumped sand all over me. They thought it was hilarious. I knew I'd made a mistake as soon as it became obvious that when sand is packed around the body, the body can't move.

If I'd suffered from claustrophobia, I would have freaked out totally. There I was, just a head sticking out of the sand. Spike caught a small crab and tried to get it to clamp onto my nose. Someone else said that he had found a fat jellyfish and that he was

going to put it on my head.

"They're poisonous, you know," I said.

"Well, don't move a muscle," he said.

Claire crouched down in front of me. She lowered her face until it was close to mine. Then she did something extraordinary. She kissed me on the lips. I was shocked, and for a moment everything I felt about her changed. I forgave her everything. But in a split second, all that vanished. She stood up, turned to her friend, and said, "There. I did it. You owe me five dollars."

Someone put a hat on my head. Then all of my friends walked away, waved back, and said loudly, "We'll come back later." They laughed and hoped, I suppose, that I would panic about being left there. But I wasn't going to give them the satisfaction.

It was only a few minutes later that I heard Claire scream, "Shark!" The kids in the water left in a hurry and raced up the beach. There was no shark. She had seen a dolphin's fin. Her panic made people nervous though, and no one came down the beach to go swimming again.

I waited for them to come and dig me out. I couldn't swivel my head around to see what was going on behind me. I heard Mr. Smith say, "All right, let's head back to the campsite." There was

silence for a few seconds after that. Then I heard his voice again, only this time it was farther away.

"Someone's left a hat on the beach."

From where he was standing, it would look like just a hat. I expected Spike or one of the others to race down and free me, but nobody came.

There was no one on the beach now but me. The hat protected me from getting sunburned. But I could not believe that my friends could do this to me. Of course, it wasn't deliberate. Claire's shark panic had probably driven all thought of me out of their minds. So they must not have heard Mr. Smith's comments about the hat. They would realize that I was missing soon enough. I calmed down and entertained myself with thoughts about how bad my friends would feel when they realized what they had done. Maybe Claire would feel sorry for me. Was it the Boulder gene that made me think that pity was a good attention-seeking strategy?

While I was pondering all this, I noticed that the arcs of spent waves were creeping closer and closer to me. I suddenly realized what being buried in damp sand meant. I struggled against the sand furiously. But I was more in danger of dislocating a shoulder than of freeing myself.

I found my voice when the first wave reached my chin. It swirled around my neck and bubbled into my mouth before withdrawing. The next wave didn't quite reach me, and neither did the next one. The fourth wave washed around me. Then I realized that it was only a matter of time before I would disappear under them. I have never yelled so loudly in my life. It was while my mouth was wide open that the next wave emptied itself down my throat. Coughing and spluttering, I continued to cry out.

It was Mr. Harrold and Mr. Smith who rescued me. I heard them calling me and then heard their footsteps pounding down the beach toward me. They were both white with horror. They dug quickly, which was just as well because just after they'd started, a wave broke that covered my head completely. I had to hold my breath until it was sucked back into the ocean.

"Roscoe!" exclaimed Mr. Smith

*pondering*: Thinking about something for a long time.

as he dragged me out of the hole. "Who is responsible for this?"

"It was my idea," I confessed. "I admit, it wasn't a very good one."

Mr. Smith's fear for my safety had passed. I could tell that now he was very angry. I suspected that the real reason for his anger was the staff's carelessness. They should have called the roll, which they hadn't done.

When I walked, with Mr. Smith and Mr. Harrold, into the camp, there was a sigh of relief and a round of applause. There must have been a few anxious moments when my absence was discovered, and they realized that the tide was coming in.

"Okay," said Mr. Smith. "As soon as you've all eaten, I want you in your tents. I don't want to hear a sound! From now on, no one had better step out of line."

# Chapter 5
# A Big Win

*Fact*: Some mathematicians calculate that a lottery player may have to spend $200,000 over time to accrue $100,000 in winnings.

THE NEXT BIG HURDLE in my life was the oral presentation we had to deliver each term.

I hate giving talks at school. Every time I'd given one in the past, something had gone wrong.

Why do they make us do these things? How is this going to help us later on? I had no idea that two minutes could be an eternity until I tried to explain why the object I had brought in was important to me. That was the theme of the talk—a favorite object. I thought I had enough material. I'd chosen a model airplane that I had made when I was six. But I ran out of things to say after exactly 30 seconds. There was this awful silence.

"Thank you, Roscoe," said Mr. Harrold. "Perhaps next time you might like to actually prepare something."

I returned to my seat, my face bright red, and accidentally sat on my model airplane. I wasn't upset. I blamed it on my humiliation.

---

When another talk was assigned, I was ready. I had a brilliant tale to tell. It was from the family chronicle, and it had everything—suspense, violence, and celebrities. Better still, it was about a member of my own family. There would be no appalling silences this time around. I intended to make sure that my fly was zipped up, my shoelaces tied, and that nothing was sticking out of my nose. Experience has taught me some things.

On the day my talk was scheduled, there were two other speakers before me. Lorraine Bell gave a talk about breeding maggots for bait, which was disgusting but a big hit. George Pandopoulos told the class about his collection of *Star Trek* memorabilia. Then he made the mistake of handing some cards around the class. Two got lost somewhere in the back row. When I got up to talk, I had to wait while Mr. Harrold removed George's hands from around Peter Spike's neck. George calmed down only when Mr. Harrold assured him that his

| |
|---|
| *appalling*: Horrifying. |

cards would be returned.

"I don't have his stupid cards," said Peter Spike.

Mr. Harrold sighed and told me to begin my talk. There was never any point arguing with Peter Spike.

"A member of my family, my great-great-great-great-grandfather was indirectly responsible for the assassination of Abraham Lincoln."

I could tell from the looks on their faces that they were interested, except for Peter Spike, who said, "Who's Abraham Lincoln?"

"Go on," said Mr. Harrold.

"On April 14, 1865, Mr. and Mrs. Lincoln went to the Ford Theatre in Washington to see a play."

"What was the name of the play?" asked Claire. She was trying to throw me off, but I knew that some troublemaker would ask this, so I was ready.

"*Our American Friend,* actually."

Claire curled her lip.

"Anyway, they got to the theater and were shown to their seats. They had a box—that's like a private viewing area. Just after they were seated, a Roscoe

> **assassination**: *A murder committed by secret attack.*

Boulder, who was in charge of the boxes that night, came into Mr. Lincoln's box. He told Mr. Lincoln that he had been shown to the wrong box and that perhaps he might be more comfortable in the correct one.

"The president's box had comfortable chairs and a better view of the stage. Mr. Lincoln thanked him and moved to the president's box. That was where John Wilkes Booth found him and shot him. If that Roscoe Boulder had left Mr. Lincoln where he was, there would have been no one in the president's box for Booth to shoot."

I paused to allow my story to sink in.

Peter Spike said, "Well, what was it, a booth or a box? I don't understand."

Before I could respond, the bell signaling a fire drill went off. Of all times, I thought, for this to happen. I was just about to explain the Roscoe Boulder phenomenon. Everyone stood up and moved toward the door. No one took fire drills seriously, but they were usually a welcome distraction.

"Interesting talk," said Mr. Harrold on his way out. "You've got quite an imagination, Roscoe."

phenomenon: *An exceptional or unusual person or event.*

It didn't occur to me immediately, but

later that day I realized that this was actually an insult. He hadn't believed a word I had said about Lincoln and Roscoe.

"That was so lame," said Claire Moore as she passed me in the hall.

I t was a few weeks after I had returned from the field trip that Mom received some extraordinary news.

"We've won a prize," she said over dinner. "What I mean is, *I* have won a prize."

I had never seen her so excited.

"Your mother has won a prize, Roscoe," confirmed my father.

I was missing something. My mother had won a prize. Big deal. People win prizes every day. Unless this was a big, big prize, like a trillion dollars, I couldn't see what all the excitement was about.

"Are we rich?" I asked.

They were puzzled by this question. It interrupted the flow of their excitement. My mother looked at me quizzically.

"No, Roscoe, we're not rich, but we are going on a vacation."

There was that excitement again.

"We, I, won a family vacation to Sandy Island. I filled in a form in the supermarket ages ago and thought no more about it. Today, I received a letter saying that I had won. Isn't that incredible?"

I'd heard of Sandy Island. It was a tropical resort island. A few kids from my class had been there. It was terrific that Mom had won, but I still didn't get why both Mom and Dad were so excited.

"That's great, Mom," I said. My voice obviously lacked the right amount of thrill. Dad said that I clearly didn't understand the significance of this event.

"Roscoe," he said, with a patient tone that I had begun to recognize as a prelude to a lecture. "There is no precedent for this in our family. I have searched through the *Chronicle*. As far as I can tell, your mother is the first Boulder, husband or wife, to win something in more

> **prelude**: Something that comes before and prepares for the main or important parts.

than 400 years." He leaned across the table and kissed Mom on the cheek.

"I entered the competition on the same day that you escaped drowning on the field trip. Now, don't tell me that this is just coincidence, Roscoe."

"Well, of course it's coincidence," I said. "I thought you didn't believe all that Boulder stuff."

"Sometimes, Roscoe, you have to stand back and marvel. Sometimes, you have to allow yourself to wonder if there might not be something in it after all. I am the first person to break the losing streak in the Boulder family. No one before me has won so much as a prize in a raffle.

"And it's not because we don't try, Roscoe. We enter raffles and competitions like everyone else. But we just accept that we're making a donation to charity. We never expect to win."

"But this was in a supermarket," I said. "How is that a donation to charity?"

"That's the remarkable thing," said Mom. "Normally, I only enter drawings when I know the money is going to a charity. This one time, I filled in a form put out by a margarine company. I had to write, in 20 words or less, why I liked their product. I'd never tried their product, but I wrote a little poem saying how splendid it was and, bingo, I won."

"What was the poem?" I asked.

"That secret will go with me to the grave. I'd be too embarrassed to tell anyone. I haven't even told your father and I never will."

"It'll probably be printed on the side of every tub of margarine, and it'll probably have your name on it," said Dad helpfully.

"There's more news, too," said Mom. "The Moores are going to be on Sandy Island at the same time. Isn't that wonderful? You and Claire will be able to hang out together. Is that the right expression?"

"Yes," I said. "That's right, but it sounds weird when you say it."

"That's because it's ugly, honey. I don't use ugly expressions unless I'm trying to communicate with teenagers."

Claire Moore and me together on a tropical island. In a novel, that might be the beginning of a great romance. There was no chance of that. I would have to find ways of avoiding her. This would be difficult because our parents would be hanging out together. I knew I couldn't rely on her to behave herself, even in front of my parents. She would say something snide and make me blush. Perhaps I should ask Dad for advice again. No. He and Mom would be watching

us then for any sign of a change in our relationship. Parents are always on the lookout for that first romance.

I decided to write Claire a letter. I could never talk to her because she was always with her friends. I wanted to tell her that I had no argument with her. And so we should try to get along, since we were going on vacation to the same place at the same time. I wrote:

Dear Claire,

I do not understand why you are so rude to me so often. I do not remember doing anything to you or saying anything about you that would be offensive. We are going to be staying in the same hotel on Sandy Island, and I think that it would be good if we could call a truce and get along. What do you think?

Roscoe

I put this letter through the air vents in the door of her locker. I regretted writing it as soon as it had disappeared. The next day there was a letter from Claire in my locker. I didn't read it until I was walking home. I was nervous about opening it. Was it possible that I had a crush on her? I had to admit to myself that this was indeed possible.

Her letter was terrible.

> Dear Loser,
>
> I am not rude to you because you can't be rude to a loser. You haven't done anything to be offensive. You just are offensive. Don't come near me on Sandy Island. I wouldn't want anyone to think that we were friends.
>
> Claire

I was so devastated by this letter that I forgot my fears about involving Mom and Dad and showed it to them. They did not react in the way that I thought they might react. They exchanged looks and burst into laughter.

"What's so funny?" I asked.

"Roscoe," said Dad. "This is classic."

"What do you mean?"

Mom said, "Honey, Claire really likes you."

I read the letter again and again. What was I missing?

Over the next few weeks, excitement in our household mounted. We hardly ever went away on vacation. When we did, we didn't go far. Mom always said it was unwise to tempt fate by taking

Dad a dangerous distance from the hospital emergency room.

This vacation, though, was different. It felt like it had been blessed in some way. The fact that it had been the result of good luck suggested to my parents that, for once, a long trip was a risk worth taking. I agreed.

I loved seeing my parents getting hyper about this vacation. They discussed the details endlessly. What should we take? Should we take sweaters? What about insect repellent? Was there malaria there?

"Mom," I said, "we're not going to the ends of the earth. This is a resort. They'll have everything we need there."

Mom packed and repacked several times.

"No, Mom. You don't need to pack six bath towels."

"I think the bag is still too heavy."

"Perhaps if you took out the ten bottles of water."

"Are you sure I won't need woolen pants?"

"Mom, it's the tropics!"

When the day finally arrived, we took a taxi to the airport. We didn't take any chances. Most people usually arrive about an hour before their flight. We calculated that three hours should give us time to deal with any Boulder occurrences and still catch the flight. Incredibly, nothing went wrong on the way to the airport, and there were no problems at the check-in. Now, all we had to do was fill in three hours. Mom insisted that we sit in one spot.

"We have to minimize the chances of accidents," she explained. "We'll all read and try to keep very still."

Now that the Boulder jinx had kicked in, we chose a spot that was well away from anything that might fall on Dad, or me. You probably think my mother was being paranoid, but you have to see this from her point of view.

This was her first real vacation. She knew only too well that trouble could strike from the most unexpected places. She figured that if we sat in the middle of the seating area, she could see any potential hazards. When Dad stood up to go to the men's room, she visibly sank into her seat. I could tell that she had decided that this was it. The vacation was over. He'd slip and break his leg, or knock himself out, or goodness knows what. When he came back in one piece, her face broke into a radiant smile.

---

**minimize**: *To reduce as much as possible.*

---

All she had to worry about then was when I went to the men's room.

On our way to board the plane, Mom put her arms around Dad and me. She said, "Life is wonderful, and this is going to be the best vacation in the history of the world."

Well, I don't know if it was the best vacation in the history of the world. But it turned out to be one of the most unusual.

# Chapter 6

# A Serpent in Paradise

*Fact*: The sea snake *Hydrophis belcheri* is the world's most venomous snake. It lives in the ocean off northwest Australia.

W E STEPPED OFF the plane onto the runway. We were hit by a blast of hot air and a sweet scent that was a mixture of tropical flowers, salt, and asphalt. The terminal was small, and there was no baggage carousel. Instead, all of the luggage was loaded onto a trailer and driven to the front of the terminal. Passengers dug around in it until they found their suitcases. There wasn't much luggage, so this wasn't as bad as it sounds.

We waited until the other passengers had collected their stuff. There were two suitcases remaining. There should have been three. Where was mine? The man at the check-in counter said that he was terribly sorry but that somehow my suitcase must have gotten lost.

This had never happened before, and he would see what he could find out. He made a phone call, nodded a few times, looked concerned, nodded some more, then hung up.

SOUTH AMERICA

Brazil

Peru

Bolivia **PARAGUAY**

Chile

Argentina

Uruguay

"I have no idea," he said, "how this could possibly have happened, but apparently your bag is on its way to Paraguay. Of course, it will be returned as soon as possible."

Paraguay? I didn't even know where that was.

"My clothes are in it. What will I wear?"

"You'll only need the shorts you're wearing," said the man. "It never gets cold here."

The first thing I thought of was that Claire would notice that I wore the same thing every day. I told myself that I had to stop thinking like that. Who cares what Claire Moore thinks? Make a mental note, I told my brain, remember to ignore Claire Moore.

Part of Mom's prize included a limousine from the airport to our hotel. When we got there, an overdressed woman greeted us. She told us that our luggage, the pieces that had arrived safely, would be placed outside our rooms. Then we were to have a complimentary drink before going on a tour of the resort. She said her name was Mandy, and she led us into Jack's Snack Bar.

Jack's was a big, open area with ceiling fans whirring overhead. It was in the shape of an octagon, and the folding doors on all sides were open. There was hardly anybody there. A young couple sipped from glasses that were crowded with small umbrellas, odd pieces of fruit, and plastic swizzle sticks. They weren't talking to each other, though. They looked like they'd just had an argument. Their drinks were festive, but their faces were strained.

"How romantic," Mom whispered. "The first argument of the honeymoon."

Mom and Dad each ordered a tropical fruit drink, and I ordered a lemonade. Mandy wandered off to supervise. When the drinks arrived, they had the same assortment of umbrellas and plastic swizzle sticks rammed into the glasses. They must go through millions of those little umbrellas.

complimentary: Given free as a courtesy or favor.

Mandy came and sat with us, and we discussed what we would do that afternoon. We

decided to take a boat out to the reef and do some snorkeling. If Mom was in any way concerned about the opportunities this offered for accidents, she didn't show it.

Mandy kept looking at her watch while we sipped our drinks. It was obvious that she didn't care too much for the role of looking after guests who had won a prize. We took the hint and gulped down the drinks. Mandy then led us on a whirlwind tour of the resort. There were four swimming pools, one of them for children only. Parents could leave their kids here, confident in the knowledge that a lifeguard was on duty at all times.

The resort was spread over a wide area. It consisted of several dining rooms and bars, game rooms, and a series of small cabins. Each of these was enclosed in its own lush garden and faced the ocean.

When we arrived at our cabin, our luggage was sitting outside the door. Or rather my parents' luggage was sitting outside the door. Mine was somewhere in South America. Mandy handed Dad what looked like a credit card and showed him how

**snorkeling**: *Swimming underwater using a snorkel, a tube that sticks out of the water, for breathing.*

to swipe it to unlock the room. Keys were considered too low-tech for the Sandy Island Resort. She smiled her big toothpaste-smile and hurried away.

Dad swiped the card and turned the handle of the door. It was locked. He swiped the card again and still the room remained closed to us. He tried turning the card upside down, then reversing it. Nothing. He wiped it on his pants (I don't know why he thought this might help) and tried yet again. Nothing.

"Let me try," I said.

I took the card and swiped it. Nothing.

"Maybe it's become demagnetized," I said, although I didn't have a clue what that meant.

"Perhaps it just needs to be de-Boulderized," Mom said. She had been waiting patiently. Now, she took the card. Dad and I folded our arms and waited to say, "I told you so." She slid the card into the slot, and a small click indicated that the door was unlocked. She looked at us and said, "It's all in the way you hold your mouth."

The accommodation was luxurious. There was a large living room with cane furniture, a kitchen, and two

> accommodation: A place to stay while traveling.

bedrooms. Each bedroom had its own bathroom and its own balcony, which looked directly onto the beach.

The sand was clean and white, and the water was the color of brilliant emeralds. A slight breeze cooled the rooms and brought with it the smell of the ocean. Looking out over the sea, I thought that nothing bad could ever happen in such a place. This was how I imagined paradise might look.

It's amazing how quickly paradise can turn into a nightmare.

I had never snorkeled on a reef before, so the afternoon of that first day was a revelation to me. I would rate it as one of the greatest experiences of my life, even though I ended up in the small hospital attached to the resort.

A motorboat took us out to the reef. There were seven or eight other guests who had also chosen this activity. There wasn't a cloud in the sky. I thought that the reef was close to the island. But we were skimming across the ocean for almost an hour before the anchor was dropped.

When I looked over the side, I could see a few fish swimming about but nothing spectacular. I was

beginning to think that the reef had been overrated. Not until I put on the goggles and snorkel and lowered myself into the water did the wonders beneath the surface reveal themselves.

As soon as I put my face underwater, my eyes were assaulted by an explosion of color and activity. The corals vibrated and shimmered as light played across their surfaces. Fish, which were lavishly colored, darted among them. No photograph could do justice to the electric charge that the first sight of the reef gave me.

There is no Eden without a serpent, and this underwater Eden was no exception. I had never heard of sea snakes, let alone seen one. Who knew that snakes could swim? That is why I got such a shock when a snake swam into my vision. It curled and coiled its way toward me, its flat

tail driving it effortlessly. This just didn't compute. So, despite the fact that I needed air, I stayed still and watched it, fascinated.

The snake was in no hurry, and it didn't seem to notice that I was even there. When it was only an arm's length from my face, I automatically raised my arm to shoo it away. I know it sounds ridiculous, to try to shoo something away underwater. But what else was I supposed to do? Would you have a better plan under the same circumstances? I don't think so.

In the process of shooing the snake away, my hand came into contact with its head. I shooed it away all right, but not before it sank its fangs into the webbing on my hand between my thumb and index finger. A thin drizzle of blood rose from the wound, dispersing like smoke.

I broke the surface and clambered into the boat. I told the operator of the boat what had happened. He took one look at my hand and signaled to the snorkelers. We had to cut the visit short and leave immediately.

I am not particularly observant, but I couldn't help noticing that the operator was more than a little concerned. I began to share his concern

clambered: Climbed awkwardly.

when I overheard one of the passengers whisper, "It was a sea snake. They're deadly."

Mom and Dad reassured me that the pressure bandage being applied was just a precaution. I don't know whether it was the toxin that had been injected into my body or the obvious nervousness of everyone around me, but I suddenly felt very ill. I vomited over the side and felt better for a minute. Then I felt sick again. I began to imagine the poison rushing through my system.

Dad tried to calm me down by telling me that panicking was the worst thing I could do. This only made me panic more. The trip back to the resort seemed to last an eternity. The island's only ambulance was waiting for me. The details of the incident had been radioed ahead. So there was no delay in identifying the venom or giving me an antivenin.

"You, young man," said the resort's doctor, "are very, very lucky. You are the first person to be bitten by a sea snake since Sandy Island was developed 30 years ago. They rarely bite people. Their fangs aren't well positioned for gripping us, you see. It's a freakish

> **antivenin:** Medicine used to treat people bitten by a poisonous snake.

accident. You were doubly lucky because they are very poisonous. But the one that bit you didn't manage to get much venom into you."

Why did he keep insisting that I was lucky? I had been bitten by a deadly snake. I had ruined everyone's snorkeling trip. And I was stuck in the hospital overnight. This did not strike me as lucky.

"It all depends on how you look at it," said Dad helpfully.

# Chapter 7

# I'll Never Eat Lobster Again

THE NEXT TWO days were uneventful. We swam and explored and laughed when we remembered that all of this was costing us nothing. Mom said that she might even buy a tub of that margarine when we got home. Dad was stung by a jellyfish and had big, red welts across his back to prove it. Apparently it was

unusual for the really poisonous species of jellyfish to be in the area at this time of year. Needless to say, if there was one about, it was bound to find Dad. He also cut his foot on a shell, almost knocked himself out with a tennis racquet (don't

ask), and ate a bad oyster, which made him nauseous.

The Moores had not yet arrived. So I had not been able to assess the situation between Claire and me in light of my parents' interpretation of her letter. I was skeptical. But they insisted that the intensity of her dislike was an obvious smoke screen to protect her from the ridicule of her friends.

"Girls," my mother had said, "are complicated creatures."

"You'd better believe it," said my father.

The Moores arrived on the third day of our vacation. I waited until dinner to tell about my first disaster. Claire had had her hair cut short, and I found myself staring at her.

"Do you like it?" she asked.

"Yes," I stammered.

That was all she said for a while. Our parents were laughing and talking. Claire and I were looking around the room.

"Look at her," she said suddenly, indicating a woman wearing a green dress with orange flowers on it.

"She thinks she looks flashy," I said. "But she just looks like a neon sign."

Claire laughed, and everything she had ever said to me was washed clean. After that we talked about teachers and how dumb some of them were.

"Don't forget ugly," she said, and we both laughed. The letter was not mentioned, and Claire was not behaving in the way her letter suggested she would behave. I began to think that I was on a roll with her. I ordered lobster for the main course. I had never tasted lobster, but I thought it was a sophisticated thing to do.

When the meal arrived, I tried to create the impression that the expensive lobster was a regular part of my diet. I picked up my fork and skewered a square of the white meat and put it in my mouth. There was none of the hesitation I would normally show when tasting food that I had never tasted before. I didn't like it much, but I chewed and swallowed with gusto.

"Do you want to try a bite?" I asked Claire.

"No thanks, I don't like fish."

I was going to point out that a lobster is not a fish, but I thought this might ruin our improving

relationship. I took another mouthful of lobster and swallowed it without chewing.

"How's the lobster?" Mom asked.

"Great," I said and polished off another forkful. How was I going to get through the whole thing? That problem was solved in an unexpected way.

I noticed an odd feeling at the back of my throat. When I swallowed, I was aware of a slight numbness. Then my lips began to tingle. The tingling sensation grew and my lips went numb.

"My gosh!" said Claire, and her hand flew to her mouth to stifle a laugh.

"What?" I said. When I spoke, the word sounded thick and muffled.

"Your lips," said Claire. "Look at Roscoe's lips!"

"Oh my gosh," said Dad.

"Oh my gosh," said Mom.

"Oh my gosh," said Mrs. Moore.

"Oh my gosh," said Mr. Moore.

I felt my lips with my fingers. They had swollen to twice their size. My mother, accustomed as she was to emergencies, took charge.

"Roscoe, can you swallow?"

67

I nodded. I didn't dare try to speak.

"Good. That means your throat isn't going to swell and close. Still, we need to get you to the hotel doctor now. You're allergic to lobster. Big time. You need an antihistamine injection. Simple."

"Can we help?" asked Mrs. Moore.

"No. It won't take long. We'll be back in no time."

Claire couldn't contain herself any longer. She burst out laughing.

"The lips! The lips!" she said. "I'm sorry, but your lips are HUGE. They look like a special effect."

I felt the full force of the jinx hit me at that moment. The first time that Claire had shown an interest in me, I'd ended up dancing in front of her, naked. Now this.

The injection of antihistamine worked quickly. But my lips remained blubbery and peculiar for the rest of the evening. I hardly said another word. I couldn't wait to get back to my room. Claire kept looking at me and giggling. So much for being sophisticated.

> antihistamine: A medicine used for treating allergic reactions.

I needn't have worried about my lips forming the

main topic of conversation the next day. The hurricane took care of that.

M om told me about the hurricane.

"All of the guests are required to meet in the dining room in three hours," she said. "There's a hurricane on the way, and it looks like a big one."

"But it's not hurricane season," I said. "Besides, the sky is absolutely clear."

"It's always hurricane season when there's a Boulder in town," she said matter-of-factly. "It's on the radar, and it's headed this way. The hotel people say that there is nothing to worry about. We'll all be quite safe. They've been through lots of them, and they know what to do."

On the way to the dining room, I noticed that the air had begun to smell of rain, and the light had become a pearly gray. The wind rose slightly and whipped some trash along the path. I looked out toward the horizon and was astonished. Huge banks of dark, boiling clouds advanced over the sea, and a great, gray dome of rain formed an arc in the distance. It was spectacularly beautiful.

The hotel staff was taping up windows when we

entered the dining room. There were lots of people there, most of whom I hadn't seen before. They must have stayed in their rooms or something. Maybe they just went out fishing every day. I had no idea so many people were staying here. The Moores were there. I saw them on the other side of the room.

Claire was with them. She pushed her lips out to make them look grotesque. Then she smiled and waved to me. I was going to walk across to her, but just as I decided to do so, I heard the sound of steady rain. The curtains in the room had not yet been drawn. Through the window, I could see what looked like a wall of rain moving toward us. It fell like a wave upon the hotel. Then a fist of wind forced its way through an unsecured door and blew paper napkins around the room.

"Is this it?" someone asked.

"No, no. This is just the advance party. The real thing won't be here for another hour or so," said a man whom I recognized as a waiter.

"We should stay together," Dad said.

> grotesque: Unnaturally odd or ugly.

I had never heard or seen such rain. It didn't ease up but poured nonstop until the full force

70

of the hurricane arrived. After that, we couldn't hear each other speak over the raging din.

I had expected to be excited. I had not expected to be afraid, but I was. The sound of the hurricane sent shivers through my body. I sat in a kind of rigid panic as the winds battered the hotel. The hideous sounds of metal moving on metal cut through the roar. The screaming and screeching of corrugated iron being torn away from roofs was a sound I would never forget. There was no letup. The wind settled into a ferocious symphony, steady and regular. It was punctuated by isolated clatters, bangs, and scrapes. Objects blew around outside or groaned their resistance to the battering.

For a few minutes, as if a switch had been thrown somewhere, there was complete silence. People stood up, and there were murmurs of relief.

"It's not over," said the waiter. "We're in the eye. It'll start again soon."

He was right. When the winds returned, it was with renewed fury as if they had gathered strength when the eye passed over us.

Three hours after it started, it was over. It was still raining and the

**corrugated**: Formed or shaped into wrinkles or folds.

wind was still blowing, but the hurricane had passed. It was safe to go outside. We opened the doors of the dining room and stepped into chaos.

There was debris lying everywhere. It was as if a giant had put his foot down right in the middle of Sandy Island. People were moving about and there were no serious injuries. But the resort was badly damaged. We joined the Moores as we walked back to our cabins. Claire had been crying. Her eyes were red and puffy. Her mother had her arm around Claire's shoulders.

Our cabin was undamaged, but the view from the windows had changed. The beautiful white beach was now strewn with branches and sheets of roofing. The ocean had dumped seaweed and lots of other junk—bottles and fishing line and boxes—on it. A small yacht had also been washed up on the beach. It was upside down. Its broken mast propped the boat up so that its stern was wedged in the sand. Its bow jutted at an angle toward the sky. It looked like a spectacular but ridiculous sculpture.

> **debris**: Scattered bits and pieces after something has been destroyed.

There was a slight problem with the bathroom. It looked okay, but nothing worked. The toilet didn't flush, the

faucets didn't work, and there was no electricity. The hotel people were amazing. They were prepared for this kind of emergency. They were able to provide a decent meal for the guests by barbecuing everything, and there was plenty of bottled water. The guests from the hotel next door ate at our hotel because the damage over there was extensive. I saw Claire Moore and went up to her to say hello.

"Have you noticed that wherever you go everything gets wrecked?" she said. That was all she said, too, because after that she turned on her heel and strutted off. I wasn't fast enough, but I should have pointed out that the same could be said of her.

We couldn't use the swimming pools to get clean because they were filled with debris. Not that we were dirty. It's just that it was pretty humid, and you get sticky really fast in those conditions. We were advised not to swim in the ocean either. The hurricane had driven large numbers of stingers into shore and getting lashed by their tentacles was not recommended for good health.

I knew it had to happen. I was still disappointed when Dad announced that the island was being evacuated the following day.

**evacuated**: Removing people from a place of danger.

Flights had been organized to the mainland. We had been assigned to a 12-seater aircraft. Mom said that that was some reward. She had never flown in such a small plane and was sure that it was going to be exciting.

When we boarded the plane the next morning, we all began the longest journey of our lives.

# Chapter 8
# The Crash

*Fact*: We are often told not to swim for an hour after eating to avoid cramps. In fact, there is no evidence to connect eating and cramps. Long-distance swimmers actually eat while they are swimming in order to avoid cramps.

THE PLANE WAS a Twin Otter. There were only six people on the plane, the Moores and us. We had agreed to wait and be the last guests to leave. Mom said that Mrs. Moore had confided to her that Claire had a fear of flying. She could deal with it better if there were fewer people on the plane. Also the fact that we were friends made a big difference. There was so much I didn't know about Claire Moore.

"Your job is to distract her, Roscoe," said Mom. "Keep her mind off the fact that we're flying. That's not going to be easy in this tiny plane, I know. You'll just have to do your best."

How was I going to keep her mind off the fact that we were flying when every seat was a window seat?

When Claire arrived, she was white-faced. She was not ashamed to admit that she was terrified of flying. I admired her for that. She sat rigid in her seat, her eyes focused on the back of her mother's head. Her clenched fingers turned white when the engines coughed into motion. Take off is the worst time, particularly in a small plane. It shakes and rattles and sounds as if the rivets holding it together are going to pop.

I tried to think of something to talk to her about. There was a Roscoe Boulder who was the first paying passenger on an aircraft. The pilot was Orville Wright. Unfortunately, the plane crashed. They were both slightly injured. This wasn't a good time to reveal to Claire that I was related to the world's first air-crash victim.

I decided instead to tell her about the Roscoe Boulder who had a flash of inspiration. He put all of his money into the stock market in 1929. Claire forced herself to pay attention. She wanted to be distracted, but I don't think she heard a word I said. Over her shoulder, I could see that the plane had taken off into a threatening sky. There was no wind, but there was a build up of clouds, the dark color of a bruise, on the horizon.

"Welcome aboard," said the pilot over the intercom. "My name is Nell, and I hope you have a

pleasant trip. We should be landing on the mainland in about 40 minutes. We'll be flying through a little turbulence, so you may experience some bumpy movement in the aircraft, but it is nothing to worry about."

Claire blanched at the mention of turbulence, and I felt uneasy, too. This airplane wasn't exactly a "Flying Fortress." But if there's one thing I've learned, it's never to fly in a plane where you can see the steering wheel and the windshield wipers.

Nell was right about the turbulence. The plane jumped as if it had been kicked in the rear. It settled almost immediately, but then it dropped suddenly before steadying. The pilot said reassuringly, "It's just the turbulence. These small airplanes will rock a bit, but I assure you it's perfectly normal."

It's easy to say that. But when the sky outside turns black and rain starts belting against the windows, grabbing the armrest with enough force to turn it to powder is a natural thing to do. I kept my eye on the pilot to watch for any signs of panic. If she stayed calm, I figured that all was under control. So there was no point in worrying.

I looked across at Dad. Incredibly, he was asleep. Mom

> turbulence: Irregular motion of air currents.

was trying to read, but she couldn't hold the book steady. She smiled at me, and the fear in my belly stopped its rise to my throat. Claire had closed her eyes and leaned forward. She was breathing deeply, using every ounce of self-control to ward off terror.

For a few minutes we had a smooth ride, and we all relaxed.

The sputter from the engines woke Dad up. They coughed and, for one heart-stopping moment, stopped altogether. The pilot fiddled with something, and the engines came back to life. I knew that we were in trouble when I saw Nell's eyes in the rearview mirror, (until then I had no idea that airplanes even had rearview mirrors). They were the eyes of a person experiencing controlled panic.

The engines sounded rough. We began to lose altitude. It wasn't a plummet, but it was an obvious dip toward the ocean below us.

"Please put on your life jackets," she said. "This is just a precaution."

Her voice was calm. I was full of admiration for her. I knew, we all knew, that we were going to crash.

"We're losing altitude," she said.

> **plummet**: To fall straight down.

"We're going to have to put down in the sea."

Until you hear words such as these, you'll never know the effect they have on you. No one screamed. No one panicked. Perhaps we were numb with fear, but there was an extraordinary calm in the aircraft. We all had time to put on life jackets. When the engines died, we steeled ourselves for the impact.

I understood later what incredible skill it took for Nell to guide the plane to the surface of the water. We hit with bone-jarring force, wheels first. It's like hitting concrete when you hit water at that speed. But the plane did not fall apart. When it came to rest, we had time to establish that no one had been hurt. I'm not sure of the sequence of the events that took place after that. I remember Dad leaping up and screaming at people that they had to get out. He threw open an emergency exit and more or less threw people out into the water. I saw him pick Claire up by her tee shirt and hurl her into the water.

In less than a minute, there were seven of us struggling to stay above the chop. It was raining, and the wind whipped saltwater at our faces. The plane sat where it was, rocking on the waves. I thought that Dad had been stupid. Surely it would have been more sensible to stay inside where it was warm and wait to be rescued. As these thoughts were forming, the cockpit filled with water. The plane tilted downward,

79

then sank without a trace. All that remained was a slick of aircraft fuel that washed against us.

The seven of us were treading water. At first it felt relatively warm. But soon I felt the chill creeping up my legs. My denim shorts were soaked and heavy. It was hard to move my legs. So I began to take the shorts off.

"No," Dad yelled. "Leave on all of your clothes, including your shoes. They'll keep you warm."

Thank goodness for the life jackets. Without them the effort to stay afloat would have been too much. We were huddled together, bobbing up and down, in the middle of nowhere.

"There's land about three and a half miles to the west," Nell said.

"We should wait here," Dad said. "They'll be searching for us. If we form a tight circle and curl up, it will help us to keep warm."

Dad had spent a lifetime experiencing every type of

emergency situation. Along the way he had acquired some very useful knowledge. Nevertheless, I instinctively knew that this was the wrong decision. I could see that we would not survive unless we started swimming.

"We should swim to shore," I said with conviction. Claire Moore's father nodded.

"Okay, Roscoe," he said. "Tell us why."

"Because it will keep us warm and because it's our best bet. We're all in danger of getting hypothermia. If we want to get out of here alive, we have to swim for it."

"He's right," Nell said.

"If we take it slowly, we can do this," I said. People, including my parents, were looking at me as if they believed that I could guide them to safety.

I had all of the lifesaving certificates in swimming. I did know what I was talking about. This was the most dangerous situation I had ever been in, but I had never felt more confident. I wished we had a rope to keep us together. But if we watched each other carefully, we could prevent anyone from floating away. The strong swimmers

hypothermia: Below-normal body temperature.

would have to resist the urge to pull away.

"Breaststroke or sidestroke," I said. "They're best for maintaining body heat. Freestyle is too tiring."

Claire's terrified voice said, "I can't swim. I'll drown."

"Nobody's going to drown," I said. "You can do this, Claire. Hang onto my belt. You won't sink. I promise. Just stay calm and everything will be all right."

We moved off toward the shore, or the place where we assumed the shore was. No one said the word "shark," but it must have been in the back of all of our minds. I regretted ever seeing *Jaws*. I kept my imagination in check and forced my brain to focus only on swimming.

The weather made the going difficult. There were moments of calm followed by gusts of wind and stinging rain. These sudden gusts drove saltwater at our faces. It felt like I was swallowing bucketsful of it. All the while, I was conscious of Claire clinging to my belt.

After an hour of swimming, we stopped to rest and check on each other. We were all completely exhausted and red-eyed. Claire's mother was showing signs of extreme fatigue. Mom kept reassuring her that we would soon get safely to shore.

"We're doing really well," Dad said. "In another hour we'll be on land. We've come this far. There's no reason why we can't keep going."

Claire Moore suddenly caved in.

"I can't go any further," she said. "I'm just too tired."

"Yes, you can, Claire," I said.

She began to shiver uncontrollably. Her core temperature was dropping dangerously low. We had to move on. Just then the ocean itself provided the motivation to swim. We found ourselves surrounded by hundreds of jellyfish. They were transparent yet visible, like ocean ghosts. They moved blindly with the current. Occasionally they propelled themselves with a push of the bell that formed their body. Their long tentacles hung beneath this clear dome. As they brushed against us, their tentacles stung any exposed flesh. The stings were like hot needles. They

**transparent**: *Fine or sheer enough to be seen through.*

were disgusting, but in a way they saved our lives.

It didn't feel like that at the time. We were too exhausted from kicking our legs and sweeping our arms through the water trying to escape the cloud of jellyfish.

Then a sudden, fierce squall bore down upon us. It almost extinguished the flickering flame of my energy. If I was feeling this bad, I could only imagine how bad the others were feeling. I couldn't surrender because I sensed that the others were depending on me. There they all were. Their faces were drawn, but they were struggling together.

Claire had let go of my belt and was floating free. Mom was sticking close to Mrs. Moore, encouraging her. Mr. Moore's face was gray with fatigue. Dad's was determined. Of all of us, Nell seemed to be coping the best. She was very fit. Her eyes, though reddened with saltwater, shone with the fierceness of her determination to survive. I caught her eye and felt some of her strength flow into me. At that moment a wave rolled under us and lifted us skyward. We all slid down its face, except for Claire, who somehow had slipped behind it. In a split second, she was separated from us and began drifting in the

**squall**: *A sudden, violent wind, often with rain.*

wrong direction. She didn't seem to notice.

"Claire!" I yelled. My voice was hoarse and had no force in it. She wouldn't have heard me. In another second, she had disappeared from view. Mrs. Moore mouthed her name frantically and headed wildly toward where she had last glimpsed her daughter.

"Stop! Claire!" I called.

I threw off my life jacket and gave it to Mom. Before anybody could stop me, I swam freestyle in what I believed was the right direction. I don't know where I got the energy that propelled me. All I knew was that this was going to be the most important 100-meters swim I had ever done.

I saw Claire's head rising and falling with the choppy motion of the ocean. She was making no effort to make her way back to the group. It was as if she had given up and had decided to allow the sea to claim her. She looked at me dully when I grabbed her life jacket.

"Help me!" I yelled.

I needed her help. I didn't have enough strength left to drag her.

"Help me! Listen to me! If you don't help me bring you back, you'll die! Do you understand? You'll die!"

She snapped out of it and began kicking her legs.

On the way back, it was actually Claire who was supporting me. I held onto her belt and let her pull me along.

We found the others in a tight circle. Dad had organized them into his curled-up, heat-saving positions. Nobody had the energy to show much excitement at our return. Mom reached out and touched me on the arm and said simply, "Roscoe." There was such relief and love in that one word. It seemed to me that my name was, after all, big enough to take pride in.

Mrs. Moore was sobbing, but there were no tears. I supposed it was because she was dehydrated. Claire looked me straight in the eye—something she had never done—and said, "Thanks."

"I see the shore!" Nell pointed, and we all strained to locate it through the rain and spray. Yes, there it was—a yellow crescent of sand with green rising behind it. A surge of energy ran through me.

"We're nearly there," I said. "We're safe."

We weren't safe, because that was when Dad spotted the fin. He swam up to me and pointed at an area to my left. No words were spoken.

> **dehydrated**: Lacking enough body fluid.

I saw it, too, cutting through the water and leaving a trail of white foam in its wake. Dad furrowed his brow. We silently agreed to say nothing about it. Now we had to get ashore as quickly as possible.

The shark did not keep its distance. Almost as if it were taunting us, it swam lazily between us and the shore. Everyone then saw the chilling wedge of its dorsal fin. The mind plays strange tricks when it is under pressure. At this moment, the story of the Roscoe Boulder who had traveled widely through Africa popped into my head.

He had come to a tragic end while on safari. He had disturbed a pride of lions and had been obliged to run for his life. To escape, he climbed a tall tree. The lions hung around the base of the tree for a while but gave up soon. With the lions safely out of the way, the leopard sitting in the top branches was able to score an easy meal.

When the shark's fin disappeared under the water,

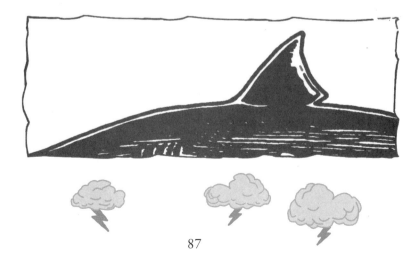

we all experienced an appalling rush of horror. It was so strong that I felt its vibration pass from one to another of us. I was sure that we each were picturing our legs dangling within the shark's sight. The hideous possibility of someone being attacked was so overwhelming that Mrs. Moore let out a scream. It curdled my blood. I had never heard a sound like this before. It came from deep within her and was almost inhuman. Perhaps it echoed beneath us because the shark did not surface.

"Let's move on," said Nell. "We're so close."

We reached an inlet where the sea was calm. There was no wind here, and the sea was not churned by currents. The chop was reduced to gentle dips and peaks. In the relative calm of this sheltered place, we began to relax. There was danger in this. I could feel my legs beginning to cramp badly. I was aware, too, that the fin was close by. Maybe it was still waiting for its chance.

"Don't stop," I urged. "Kick hard now."

As we approached the beach, the task became easier. The gentle breakers carried us over a reef and deposited us in water that was waist deep. We stumbled ashore as the sun burst through the clouds. If you read this in a story, you'd think it was corny.

I tried to stand. But my legs gave way, and I fell

forward into the sand. Claire fell, too, and so did Mom and Mr. Moore. Nell, Mrs. Moore, and Dad stood for a moment, then knelt and bowed their heads. I don't know if they were praying. But I guess that if you believed in that sort of thing there was no better time to do it.

Dad leaned over me a few minutes later and said hoarsely, "Roscoe, I'm proud to be your father."

I rolled over onto my back and smiled at him. Over his shoulder a man I had never seen before appeared. He said, "My gosh. What happened to you people?"

# Chapter 9
# The Unwilling Hero

I HATE FUSS. There was fuss. Major fuss. Newspapers, TV, the works. They all tried to turn me into some kind of hero. I was embarrassed. Claire said that I had saved her life, and it was written up as if I had done it single-handedly. I tried to tell people that we were all heroes. But that only made them write that I was a modest hero, which seemed to be their favorite kind.

The night of our rescue, we were kept in the hospital for observation. We were all fine. A strange thing began to happen to each of us, though. We began to peel. This wasn't peeling like after sunburn. This was a total skin peel, from head to foot. The doctors thought it must have been because we had

90

come into contact with airplane fuel. It looked really weird, sort of like a snake when it's shedding its skin.

All of our lives were changed by the crash. But if you think that Claire and I finally got together, well, that only happens in fiction. We became friends, but she started dating George Pandopoulos. How freaky is that? I thought she had some taste.

I realized that all Claire and I had in common was the story of how we survived. It was a great experience, and I'm glad I shared it with her. There was nothing to be gained by pretending that we had to be anything more than friends because of it. In fact, there was an awful lot to lose.

In our household, life went back to normal. Dad fell off a ladder and sprained his wrist. Mom patiently put his dinner in the oven. There was something different, though. Now I believed that whatever I chose to do in life, it would work out for the best.

The time seemed right for me to record this part of my story. I wanted it to be ready when it was my turn to write in the chronicle. I picked up my pen and I wrote, "Roscoe Boulder. That's my name. Roscoe. Boulder."

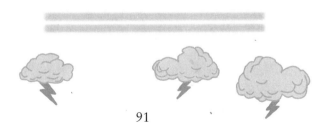

# Amazing Facts

The tomb of Egypt's boy king, Tutankhamun, is said to have been cursed. Whoever removed its treasures would die. The English Earl of Carnarvon died after removing treasures from the tomb. At the exact moment Carnarvon died, his dog died in England. The Curse of Tutankhamun or just a coincidence?

According to the *Guinness Book of Records*, Glynn Wolfe of California has been married 28 times since his first marriage in 1927.

Pro golfer Mac McClendon was having a bad day at the 1979 Masters Tournament. He told his wife that he would end up hitting someone with a ball. The next day he teed off, and the ball went into the crowd and hit his wife.

On December 5, 1664, a boat sank in the Irish Sea. Only one passenger escaped, a man named Hugh Williams. Another ship

sank in the same place in 1785. The only passenger to escape was a man named Hugh Williams. In 1820, yet another ship sank in the same place. The only survivor was named Hugh Williams.

When Gregory Riffi jumped from a helicopter in France in 1992, his bungee stretched to 2,000 feet!

In an ocean-life aquarium in Portsmouth, England, a shark leaped out of its tank—twice! The height of the tank walls had to be increased.

Abraham Lincoln was shot while watching a play in the Ford Theater. John Kennedy was shot while driving in a Ford Lincoln car.

George Dawson has survived three shipwrecks. Incredibly, on two of those occasions he was shipwrecked with a fireman named Alexander Grant.

In 1901, a man was struck twice by lightning on the same day. He was 5,250 feet underground in a gold mine, and he survived.

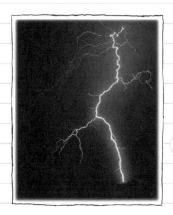

# Where to from Here?

You've just read the action-packed story of Roscoe Boulder and how he worked his way through his family's "jinx." He even became a hero. Here are some ideas for finding more stories about surviving against the odds.

## The Library

Some books you might enjoy include:
- *Hatchet* by Gary Paulsen
- *Free Fall* by Joyce Sweeney
- *White Water* by P. J. Petersen
- *The Maze* by Will Hobbs

Here's a nonfiction book to try:
*True Survival Stories* by Anthony Masters

## TV, Film, and Video

Check TV listings and ask at a video store or at your library for films about survival. Some suggestions are:
- *Swiss Family Robinson*
- *Island of the Blue Dolphins*

## The Internet

Search the Internet, using keywords such as *superstition, omen, bad luck, jinx.*

## People and Places

Local and national newspapers and newsmagazines often carry amazing stories of endurance and survival. You might also ask friends and relatives if they know of any amazing survival stories.

## The Ultimate Nonfiction Book

Be sure to check out *One in a Million*, the companion volume to *Not a Chance. One in a Million* tells you real-life stories about amazing coincidences and people who survived against the odds.

*Decide for yourself*
      *where fiction stops*
              *and fact begins.*